THE TALE OF
TOM KITTEN
AND
JEMIMA
PUDDLE-DUCK

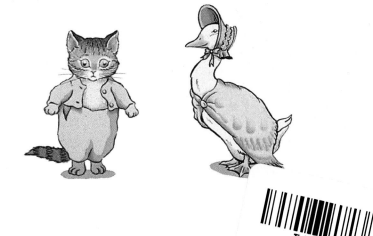

From the authorized animated series
based on the original tales
BY **BEATRIX POTTER**™

F.WARNE & CO

Once upon a time there were three little kittens and their names were Mittens, Tom Kitten and Moppet.

They had dear little coats of their own; and they tumbled about the door-step and played in the dust.

'I do wish Mrs Twitchit would keep her kittens in order,' quacked Jemima Puddle-duck.

One day their mother, Mrs Tabitha Twitchit, expected friends to tea, so she fetched the kittens indoors to wash and dress them before the fine company arrived.

4

'Goodness me, Tom, I had not realised *quite* how you have grown. Oh dear, oh dear!,' sighed Mrs Tabitha Twitchit. 'We'll just have to see what we can do.'

'Now, you must walk on your hind legs and keep away
from the dirty ash-pit. And from the pigstye - oh, *and* the
Puddle-ducks,' said Mrs Tabitha Twitchit.

  Then she let the kittens out to play in the garden while
she got the tea ready.

'Ooh, let's climb up the rockery and sit on the garden wall,' suggested Moppet.

Moppet's white tucker fell down into the road. 'Never mind,' she said, 'we can fetch it later. Now, where's Tom?'

'Come along, Tom, hurry yourself up.'

Tom was all in pieces when he reached the top of the wall;
his hat fell off and the rest of his buttons burst.

While Moppet and Mittens tried to pull him together,
there was a pit pat paddle-pat! and the three Puddle-ducks
came along the road.

'Rather fetching, don't you agree, Jemima?' asked
Rebeccah as she tried on the hat.

　Mittens laughed so much she fell off the wall. Moppet
and Tom followed her down.

'Come, Mr Drake Puddle-duck,' said Moppet. 'Come and help me to dress Tom. Come and button him up.'

But Mr Drake put Tom's clothes on *himself.*

'It's a very fine morning,' he said. And he and Jemima and Rebeccah Puddle-duck set off up the road.

Then Mrs Tabitha Twitchit came down the garden and found her kittens on the wall with no clothes on.

'My friends will arrive in a moment,' she said, 'and you are not fit to be seen – I am *affronted*.'

'Straight to your room and not one sound do I wish to hear,' she ordered.

I'm afraid to say Mrs Tabitha Twitchit told her friends that the kittens were in bed with measles.

'Dear, dear. What a shame. The poor little souls,' exclaimed Henrietta.

But the kittens were not in bed; not in the least.

'You *did* say they were poorly, didn't you, Tabitha dear?'
asked Cousin Ribby.

As for the Puddle-ducks, they went into a pond.

The clothes all came off because there were no buttons.
And they have been looking for them ever since.

But Jemima was no better at finding things than she was
at hiding them. She tried to hide her eggs, but they were
always found and carried off. No-one believed Jemima
had the patience to sit on her eggs.

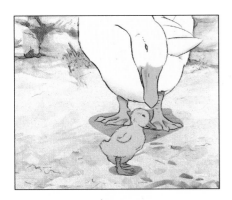

She became quite desperate.

'I *will* hatch my own eggs, if I have to make a nest right away from the farm.'

And so, one fine afternoon, Jemima set off.

Jemima was startled to find an elegantly dressed gentleman reading a newspaper.

'Madam, have you lost your way?' he enquired.

Jemima explained that she was looking for a convenient dry nesting place.

'Indeed! How interesting! A nest – but there is no
difficulty. I have a sackful of feathers in my wood-shed,'
said the bushy long-tailed gentleman.

'Goodness,' thought Jemima, 'I've never *seen* so many feathers in one place. Very comfortable, though, and perfect for making my nest, so warm . . . so dry.'

The sandy-whiskered gentleman promised to take great care
of Jemima's nest until she came back again the next day.
  'Nothing I love better than eggs and ducklings. I should
be *proud* to see a fine nestful in my wood-shed.'

At last Jemima told the gentleman she was ready to sit on her eggs until they hatched.

'Madam,' he said, 'before you commence your tedious sitting, let us have a dinner party all to ourselves. May I ask you to bring some herbs from the farm garden to make, er . . . a savoury omelette?'

Jemima Puddle-duck was a simpleton; she quite
unsuspectingly went round nibbling snippets off all the
different sorts of herbs that are used for stuffing roast duck.

'What are you doing with those onions?' asked Kep, the collie dog. 'Where do you go every afternoon by yourself?'
   Jemima told him the whole story.

Jemima went up the cart-road for the last time and flew over the wood.

The bushy long-tailed gentleman was waiting for her. 'Come in the house as soon as you have looked at your eggs,' he ordered.

While Jemima was inside she heard pattering feet round the
back of the shed. She became much alarmed.

A moment afterwards there were most awful noises -
barking, baying, growls and howls, squealing and groans.

'And I think that's the last we shall see of that foxy-
whiskered gentleman,' said Kep.

Unfortunately the puppies gobbled up all Jemima's eggs
before Kep could stop them.

'There, there, Jemima,' comforted Kep, 'I'm afraid it's just
in the nature of things – best make our way home to the
farmyard, where you belong, my dear.'

Jemima laid some more eggs in June; but only four of them
hatched. She said that it was because of her nerves, but
she had always been a bad sitter.